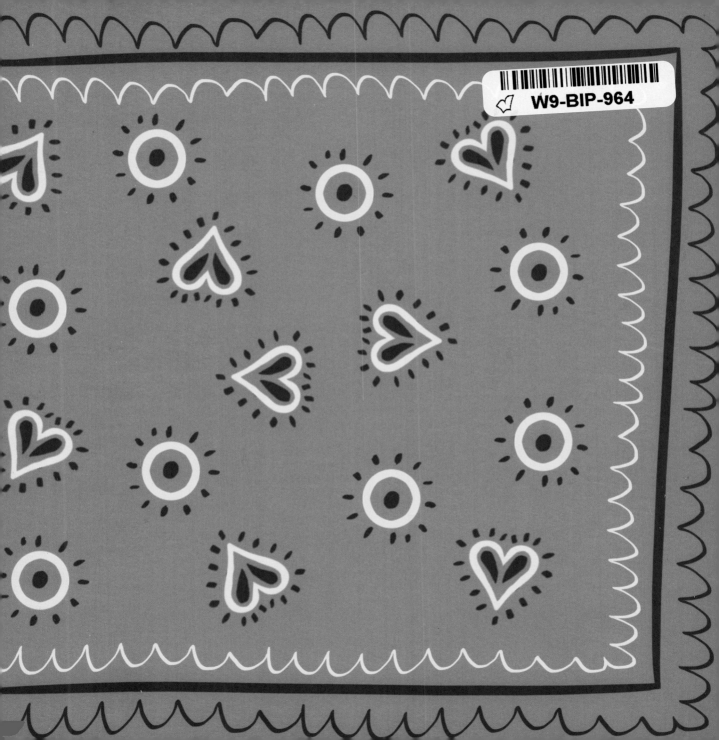

A GIFT FOR:

_____

FROM:

_____

How to Use Your Interactive Story Buddy®:

1. Activate your Story Buddy by pressing the "On / Off" button on the ear.

2. Read the story aloud in a quiet place. Speak in a clear voice when you see the highlighted phrases.

3. Listen to your Story Buddy respond with several different phrases throughout the book.

Clarity and speed of reading affect the way Cassidy™ responds. She may not always respond to young children.

Watch for even more Interactive Story Buddy characters.
For more information, visit us on the Web at Hallmark.com/StoryBuddy.

Published by Hallmark Gift Books, a division of Hallmark Cards, Inc.,
Kansas City, MO 64141. Visit us on the Web at Hallmark.com.

Editorial Director: Carrie Bolin
Editor: Emily Osborn
Art Director: Jan Mastin
Designer: Scott Swanson
Production Artist: Dan Horton

ISBN: 978-1-59530-592-3
PSB4119

Printed and bound in China
APR13

™ Hallmark's **I Reply Technology** brings your Story Buddy® to life! When you read the key phrases out loud, your Story Buddy gives a variety of responses, so each time you read feels as magical as the first.

I Reply TECHNOLOGY

BOOK 1

CASSIDY

AND THE RAINY RIVER RESCUE

By Keely Chace . Illustrated by Nikki Dyson

Hallmark

It was late afternoon on Curly Q Ranch. The day was winding down. Shadows were getting as long as a rattlesnake's necktie, and the cowboys were bringing in the herd. Cassidy looked up when she heard them singing. It was such a good ol' song, Cassidy had a hankering to join in!

Cassidy's friend Ranger saw her and trotted over.
"Howdy, Ranger!" said Cassidy. "You look thirsty!
How about a race to the watering hole?"

Ranger grinned like a coyote and took off running.
"You're on!" he shouted. "Giddyup, Cassidy!"

Even with a head start, Ranger was no match for Cassidy. She reached the watering hole in a flash and had time for a long drink before he caught up.

Out of breath, Ranger said, "You win . . . again. But there's more . . . to ranch life . . . than being fast."

Cassidy just smiled and nuzzled a duckling swimming by. She sure loved little critters—almost as much as she loved running.

Just then, Cassidy heard someone calling her: "Cassidy, where are you?"

Sure enough, Cassidy's girl was waiting for her . . . with an apple! Cassidy's legs shook with happiness. This was the best part of her day.

The girl led Cassidy into the barn and took her time grooming and feeding her pony. A few times, the girl shook her head and asked Cassidy how she got so tangled and dusty, but she always asked with a smile.

And before the girl left, she hugged Cassidy and said, "You're the best pony ever."

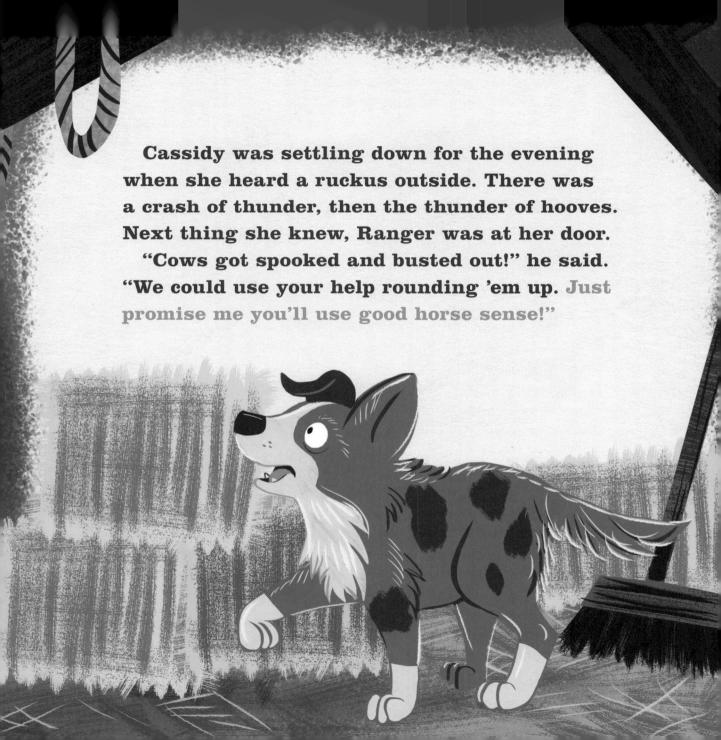

Cassidy was settling down for the evening when she heard a ruckus outside. There was a crash of thunder, then the thunder of hooves. Next thing she knew, Ranger was at her door.

"Cows got spooked and busted out!" he said. "We could use your help rounding 'em up. Just promise me you'll use good horse sense!"

Thunder boomed again as Ranger and Cassidy raced outside. Cattle were running every which way. The cowboys were doing their best to round 'em up, but there were a lot!

Ranger took off running. Cassidy reckoned it was time she got to work, too. This was going to be more fun than a barrel of horned toads!

Cassidy ran up to a white cow and said, "Howdy! Time to head on back to the herd now." But the white cow just mooed and kept running.

Then a cowboy rode by on his big black horse. It snorted and said, "No, you got it all wrong, little pony. You've got to show cows who's boss! Like this!"

The black horse galloped ahead. It caught up to the white cow and bumped it back to the herd.

Cassidy wasn't happy about that.

Cassidy tried again. Quick as lightning, she galloped up to a spotted cow. She called the cow ma'am and asked her pretty please to follow her back to the herd. It was no good.

This cow wouldn't listen to Cassidy, either. Then
Ranger ran up, looking tougher than saddle leather.
When he barked, that spotted cow MOVED!

Poor Cassidy! She didn't have the heart to be so
rough and tough.

Before long, the herd was gathered. The cows were calm. Big raindrops were falling. Cassidy kicked at a rock and sighed. She hadn't been a lick of help.

Suddenly, the quiet broke. Cassidy's ears perked up at someone sounding mighty upset.

"My baby! My baby!" a brown cow cried. "Somebody find my baby!"

The brown cow tried to break away from the herd, but the big black horse turned her right back. The brown cow mooed like her heart was breaking.

Cassidy could tell there was no time to dillydally!

Cassidy took off the way the cow had gone. Ranger chased
after her. She was heading for the river—so fast she nearly
sailed over the bank into the water.

Ranger stopped short beside her. Cassidy sniffed the wind.
She turned her ears toward a sound. Then she saw something.
It was a brown calf all alone out in the river. It looked scared
and helpless. Ranger saw the calf, too, and barked, but the
little cow was frightened.

"Let me try," said Cassidy.

Now maybe Cassidy couldn't move big cows, but she knew just how to handle a little calf. She waded into the water slowly. The calf watched her but didn't move away. When Cassidy reached the calf, she nuzzled it and spoke to it softly. In no time, the calf relaxed and let Cassidy guide it to shore.

That little pony had done it!

Cassidy led the calf back up the bank to its mama. The cowboys looked mighty surprised to see the little pony bringing in a calf.

"My baby!" said the brown cow. "Oh, thank you! Thank you!"
Ranger grinned at Cassidy. "Way to use good horse sense!"

Cassidy, Ranger, and the cowboys brought the herd home. The rain slowed down, then stopped. Cassidy spotted her girl on the fence and ran to her. The girl stroked Cassidy's nose.

"Are the cattle all in?" the girl asked a passing cowboy.
"Yes, Miss, every last one . . . thanks to this little pony."
The cowboy shut the gate and sauntered off, singing a
lonesome cowboy song. Cassidy had a hankering to join in!

The clouds parted and a big silver moon peeked through, lighting up Curly Q Ranch. Cassidy's girl hugged her and whispered the words she always said: "Cassidy, you're the best pony ever."

Have you enjoyed
reading with

CASSIDY?™

We would love to
hear from you!

Please send your
comments to:
Hallmark Book Feedback
P.O. Box 419034
Mail Drop 215
Kansas City, MO 64141

Or e-mail us at:
booknotes@hallmark.com

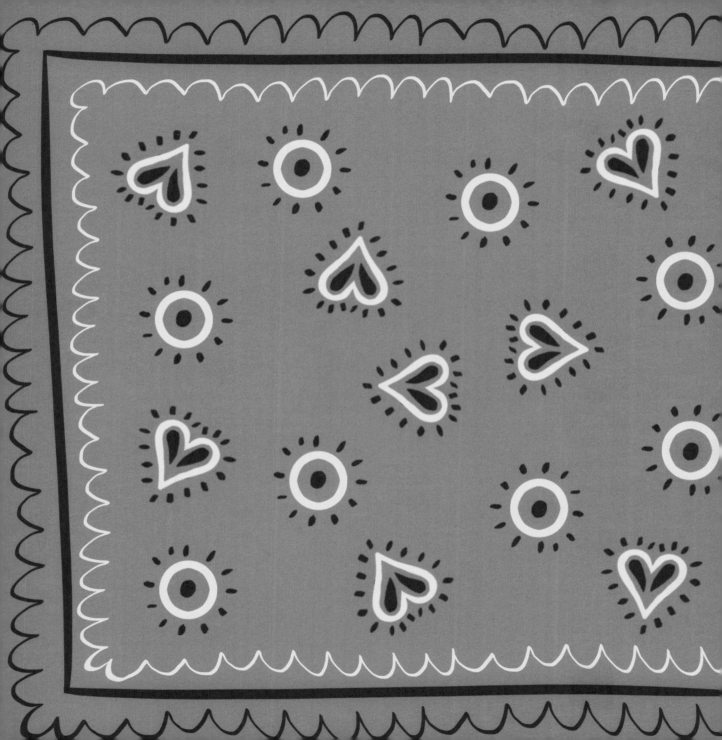